Emily Thuysbaert

Is a dyslexic author. In 2016 she challenged herself to write her first children's book.

Mia - My Incredible Adventures in Looe

Emily's books are all interactive and are inspired by her Siberian Husky Mia who has magical powers.

Emily's mission is to help children dream big dreams and to challenge the misconceptions around dyslexia by sharing her journey at national events as well as international.

Emily Thuysbaert © 2019

Books written by Emily Thuysbaert:

Mia - My Incredible Adventures in Looe © 2018
Mia - My Incredible Adventures on the Titanic © 2019
Lady the Lady Bug © 2019

All illustrations are done by Pat Thuysbaert from ©Patsartbox

If you would like to follow or contact Emily Thuysbaert

E-mail: myincredibleadventures@outlook.com
www.facebook.com/myincredibleadventures

I am Lady the Ladybug!!

I am the kindest, most caring bug you will ever meet.
But for some strange reason I always compare
what I do to everyone else.

I feel very different to all
the other Ladybugs.
I think the main reason
is I struggle to read,
write and spell.

I am told I have
something called DYSLEXIA!

It comes with gifts that I have to
find and unlock

To encourage myself to keep trying at all I do, I chant these words
over and over again.
"Never give up, Never give in"
"Never give up, Never give in"
"Never give up, Never give in"

I have the best family I could ever wish for. My mum, dad and brother are all very supportive; they encourage me to dream big dreams.

But I am very much like my dad, he to struggles to read, write and spell just like me.
They say I have inherited the Dyslexia from him. It is nice to know that someone else is like me and I am not alone in my struggles.

My dad is the famous champion Ladybug!

He tells the best stories,
all about the different battles
he has been in.

I just love listening to them.

Each time dad won a battle he
was awarded a battle spot.
There are in total six battle
spots on dad's shell.

I wish i was just as brave as
him so I could win my own
set of battle spots.

That is my dream!!

Outside my
bedroom window
I hear lots of voices;
more Ladybug
families have started
to return to the town
Loveliness up in
the tree canopy.

They must have finished
setting up the arena.
I quickly lock away my
battle suit, so no one can
see what I have planned.

As the annual tournament draws closer I can feel the excitment in the air as Ladybugs are busy getting everything set up.

Everyone is gossiping about who the contestants will be facing in the arena.

Many different animals enter this contest but only the best fighters are ever selected.

The fighters are challenged to out smart each other to win.

I have always dreamed about entering but there is only one problem, only men are allowed to enter the tournaments.

CONTESTANTS

"WOODY"

"SHADOW"

"STICKY"

WHOEVER DARES WINS
SIX BATTLE SPOTS TO WIN!

"ROBBIE"

"SHIMMER"

"EYES"

I am a very creative Ladybug;
one of my gifts I have
discovered is making things.

To enter the tournament I
need a disguise so I set about
making myself a battle
suit to hide my identity.

I will become Manny the
Ladybug!

I had spent weeks studying the different fighters and had come up with a plan of how to out smart them all.

Each opponent did something unqiue and because of my powers of observation, I now know what weapons I need to make.

All I need to do now is enter the library, books are not my friend.

The words sometimes blur and just don't make sense, but I need to make them my friend they hold the key to all knowledge, I just hope there are pictures to help me make the connection to the words I am speaking.

Dyslexia is like a maze that never ends!

Inside the arena I see Woody enter;
I know his hidden talent as I have been
watching him.
As Woody roles into his ball,
I pull out the tennis racket I have
made and I draw back my arm,
I knock Woody out of the
arena far into the
distance.

The crowd goes wild and
I hear over the speakers

"Congratulations you are
a WINNER"

With a bounce in my step I wait for my next opponent to arrive, a cold sweat starts to form as I see Shadow enter I really don't like Earwigs they look like mini scorpions!

I know from my observations he will try to get me with his pinchers I must be quick.

I pull out the Lasso I have made swinging it high above my head.

It's a miracle the lasso catches his pinchers and I pull them shut fast, jumping onto his back.

I am onto a winning streak; here's hoping my luck doesn't run out! Sticky arrives he is a tricky customer.

I have learnt he can make silk for his web which is either sticky or non-sticky.

My boots are specially made to allow me to walk across the web and to cut it!

He is expecting me to get stuck so I move fast cutting the web from underneath him. Sticky falls through!

He spins his silk attaching it to the web to stop himself from falling. I cut the thread with my boot.

Sticky falls to the arena floor with a thump!

I am so excited, I work out I have won three battle spots so far.

A trumpet sounds signalling a new contestant is ready. I quickly prepare myself for the next battle.

Robbie the robber fly is already swinging on his bar trying to scare me. But it doesn't work I know he has a blind spot. He can only swing forwards.

I act quickly and move behind him before he can grab me.

I pull out the web, I had taken from Sticky and I tangle him up so he can't move

The crowd are so loud as I hear "WINNER" ringing in my ear.

My dreams are coming true before my eyes only two more battles and I will be a champion just like my dad.

"Don't lose focus Lady" I say to myself as I watch a giant dragonfly enter the arena.

I have watched her from a distance but she is so much larger this close up.

My confidence starts to waver.

The voice in my head says **"Never give up, Never give in"**

Shimmer turns on her invisibility and I know I have one shot at getting her. Every time she turns left I can see her, she has a fault in her invisibility!

I throw the homemade glue i've made over her and the invisibility falters, she gets stuck in mid air!!

Once the cheering starts to calm down I hear a loud buzzing noise, I look up and see Eyes the wasp. The one contestant I have been worried about fighting, as I just don't know if what I have made will work on him.

He hypnotises fighters by spinning his colourful eyes.

I quickly close my eyes and put on the googles I have made.

It's now or never I open my eyes, he is face to face, his eyes are spinning but nothing!

The googles worked

"WINNER!!" is shouted over the speaker

But no one cheers we are all frozen in fear!

Thousands of birds are head in an attempt to starts screaming!!! will be no use. I start faster and faster

heading our way, the crowd I hold my arms above my shield myself. But I know it to chant my chant. Getting and louder and louder.

"NEVER GIVE UP"

"NEVER GIVE IN"

Then something magical happens

I EXPLODE!!

The birds are all shot back by the explosion; they fly away with their tail feathers on fire!

When the smoke clears I am visible for all to see, I have beautiful blue feathered wings and multiple shimmering colours coming out from my body!

I am a LADY BIRD!

gasps start to echo around the arena as people start to realise.

That Manny had actually been Lady in the Tournament winning all the battle spots.

Lady could hear the whispers from the crowd.

"Oh my it's Lady"

"Ladies aren't allowed in the tournaments"

"No way thats Lady"

The royal trumpets sound making Lady jump. "Oh no King Kai is on his way" says Lady.

As King Kai approaches, Lady bends to one knee. "Please stand Lady" says the King.

"Even though you have tricked us all, I must say your are a genius! If it wasn't for you and your ability to think outside the box, all the Ladybugs of Loveliness would be destroyed now" Explains the King.

"For saving us all I am awarding you my royal crested shell with all the battles you won today"

Lady can't believe that all her hard work and determination has made her dreams come true!

WHERE'S MIA???

All these images of Mia have been hidden throughout the book!

Can you find them?

@Looeartwork
@myincredibleadventures

e: PatsArtBox@yahoo.co.uk
w: www.PatsArtBox.co.uk
t: +44 (0)1503 262796

 Mia Publications